LIBRARIES NI
WITHDRAWN FROM STOCK
D0835686

Leonie Lord
THE Giggle Pigs
ALISON GREEN BOOKS

These are the **Giggle Pigs.**

They are always going on daring adventures and intrepid explorations.

You must never ever get the giggles.

Right now, the **four** little Giggle Pigs
are going to canoe down a
wild river.

But this is no **ordinary** river . . .

It's a river of **custard!**

And the custard turns all **lumpy**,
and the boat goes **bumpy-bumpy!**

And **this** little pig
gets the giggles
– uh-oh!

Giggle-SNORT!

Giggle-SNORT!

Off you go home.

Then **three** little Giggle Pigs
set off to climb a **mountain.**
But this is no **ordinary**
mountain . . .

It's a mountain of
underwear!

And the underwear's
quite **frilly,**

and it makes the pigs
look **silly.**

And **this** little pig
gets the giggles
– uh-oh!

Giggle-SNORT!

Giggle-SNORT!

Off you go home.

Now **two** little Giggle Pigs
go exploring in a **swamp.**
But this is no **ordinary**
swamp . . .

It's the Secret Swamp of

burps!

And the pigs go
squelchy-squelchy,
and the swamp goes
belchy-belchy!

And **this** little pig gets the giggles
– uh-oh!

Giggle-SNORT!

Giggle-SNORT!

Off you go home.

At bedtime,
one little Giggle Pig
goes on a daring quest in a castle
all by herself. It's a castle haunted by

GHOSTS!

But these are no **ordinary** ghosts . . .

These are **tickle ghosts!**

And the ghosts swoop down quite **quickly**,
and their hands are really . . .

TICKLY!

And **this** little pig
gets the giggles
– uh-oh!

Giggle-SNORT!
Giggle-SNORT!
Off she goes home . . .

. . . out of the
spooky castle,

back through the
swamp of burps,

round the mountain of
underwear,

over the river
of custard, till . . .

. . . she gets lost in a fog!

Oh, pooh!

This is no **ordinary** fog.

It's a deadly fog of . . .

bottom parps!

And this little pig doesn't
get the giggles **at all.**

But someone else does . . .
Giggle
Parp!
That was you!

giggle parp!
giggle Parp!
NO! It was YOU!
NO! It was . . .

"ALL OF US!"

And they went . . .

Tee Hee Hee
Wee Wee Wee

all the way . . .

. . . home!

Snort
Parp!
Snore

For Taylor

First published in the UK in 2019 by
Alison Green Books
An imprint of Scholastic Children's Books
Euston House, 24 Eversholt Street
London NW1 1DB
A division of Scholastic Ltd
www.scholastic.co.uk
London – New York – Toronto – Sydney – Auckland
Mexico City – New Delhi – Hong Kong

HB ISBN: 978 1 407171 95 1
PB ISBN: 978 1 407171 96 8

Designed by Zoë Tucker
Printed in Malaysia

1 3 5 7 9 8 6 4 2

Papers used by Scholastic Children's Books are made
from wood grown in sustainable forests.